Bigfoot Angel

Bigfoot Angel

A Mysterious World

CHARLES S. BREWER

iUniverse, Inc.

New York   Bloomington

Bigfoot Angel

iUniverse books may be ordered through booksellers or by contacting:

iUniverse
1663 Liberty Drive
Bloomington, IN 47403
www.iuniverse.com
1-800-Authors (1-800-288-4677)

Because of the dynamic nature of the Internet, any Web addresses or links contained in this book may have changed since publication and may no longer be valid. The views expressed in this work are solely those of the author and do not necessarily reflect the views of the publisher, and the publisher hereby disclaims any responsibility for them.

ISBN: 978-1-4401-3788-4 (pbk)
ISBN: 978-1-4401-3791-4 (ebk)

Printed in the United States of America

iUniverse rev. date: 8/3/2009

In memory of my daughter, Virgia Antle, who said, "Papa, write down you Dreams!"

Friends

The handcuffs were hurting my wrists but I kept running them up and down on the jagged piece of rock before me. I hurt all over. My arms were bruised and bloody. One eye was completely closed and I could see very little out of the other. I kept running the handcuffs up and down on the edge of the rock, with all the strength I had. My chest and back were really hurting. The pain was almost too much, but I had to get my hands free.

Someone or somebody had really worked me over. They had nearly beat me to death. Why? I couldn't remember. I knew I had to get away. Where was I? I looked around as best I could. I was in a canyon with cliffs on both sides; among pine trees and rocks. My work on the handcuffs was paying off. But then I heard a funny sound, almost like a whistle. I listened. I knew someone was behind me. I slowly turned around and there stood an enormous being. Bigfoot I thought. He was taller than my six feet by at least eight or ten inches. He cocked his head from side to side and watched me. I turned and once more worked on the cuffs. Success! I turned and there he was again. He was still watching me.

He held out his hands and made a whistling sound as if he were trying to talk to me. Then I saw he had a steel trap on his left hand. Holding out his left hand he nodded his head. I decided to get the trap off his hand. What should I do? I looked at the trap. It was a number two Coyote trap. If I tried to squeeze the ears shut so the trap would open I wouldn't have the strength to spring the trap. Bigfoot put his right hand out and took my arm between my elbow and shoulder and gently squeezed. He kept on doing this so I used my right hand and squeezed his arm. He whistled and smiled like he had just found a friend. We went over to a big flat rock and I showed him how to put his left hand down flat on the rock so the trap was in an upright position. When I got on the ears of the trap with both feet, the trap opened and he was free! He whistled, laughed, rolled on the ground and did flips. We squeezed each others arms. We had became friends.

Looking around, I saw there had been a camp here but now it was torn to pieces. The tent in shreds - food, boxes and camp gear were strewn all over. I walked through it looking for something I could use but everything was smashed. I saw two suitcases, a big one and a small one. I pulled them up, thinking they may have had something in them that I could use. I opened one of them. Bigfoot started whistling and pointing. Something was wrong. He was headed straight for the cliff and wanted me to follow him. We got behind some rocks and started walking up the face of the cliff. We had gone about two hundred yards when I played out. Bigfoot stopped under an outcrop. We could see two men walking toward the campsite--walking quietly, moving from tree to tree. Bigfoot picked up a rock and threw it in the tree tops. I had never seen anyone throw a rock like that. It was like a bullet, knocking the limbs off the trees. It frightened the men. They stopped suddenly. I could see that one of the men was wearing a badge. Bigfoot threw another rock. It whistled through the trees and more limbs fell. The men turned, looked all around and started toward the camp again. I knew Bigfoot could kill both men very easily with a rock. I looked at him; he was all puffed up like a balloon. His neck was big. His chest was enormous as he let out a terrifying scream. The echoes made my hair stand on end and the two men ran in the opposite direction as fast as they could and were soon out of sight. I squeezed Bigfoot's arm and he squeezed mine. Couldn't leave the suitcase behind, so I tied a rope securely around the handle of the suitcase and attached the other end to my belt and we started up the cliff. We were climbing higher and higher and I was getting very tired. I needed something to eat and some way of taking care of my wounds. We stopped and I sat down against the cliff. I don't know if I fell asleep or passed out.

Earl

When I woke up, there was a ringing in my ears. I was on my back in a cave beside a big blacksmith anvil which was in the center of the cave. Bigfoot was hitting the anvil with a hammer. The cave was large and it looked as if it was lit up by sun light. Bigfoot hit the anvil three times, stopped, waited for a moment, then hit it three more times. When I sat up I could see several others like Bigfoot coming from all directions toward the anvil. They came rushing at me and I just knew I was a goner. My friend stopped them and started to talk to them in that whistling talk. They understood and listened as he lifted up his hand and turned to me to help me stand on my feet. He squeezed my arm. The Bigfeet around me were at least seven feet tall or more so I assumed my friend was a teenager. Since my friend looked like some one I knew by the name of Earl, I called him Earl. These Bigfeet were beautiful, clean, well groomed and many had long black and blond hair on most of their body. Others were reddish in color. The leader was a big red haired male and his mate was blond. From what I had observed, they were the parents of Earl. There were several others and they all watched me very closely. Earl kept swinging his arms and pointing and talking in that whistling sound. Then the leader; whom I thought may be the king, came up to me and squeezed my arm between the elbow and shoulder. They all seemed very happy. We squeezed each others arms. Earl and others were trying to take off my clothes which made me feel very uncomfortable. I held up my hands to stop them and started taking off my own clothes. I had a hard time taking my boots off; got my pants off, but kept my shorts on. I really was a mess. I was beaten and bruised all over. Earl took me by the hand and we walked to the most beautiful lake that I had ever seen. It was located in the cave. It was blue with light shining from above. Earl wanted me to get in the lake. I put my foot in the water, which felt warm. Then I simply melted into the water. I had never felt anything like this--it felt so good. I lay in the water with just my nose sticking out. This was heaven. The longer I stayed in the water the better I felt, but where was I and who was I? I just couldn't remember. Oh well, better heal my body. Boy, was I hungry. I needed something to eat. I wondered what kind of food the Bigfeet ate? They were big and strong. They must have some food around here somewhere. When I looked up I could see light coming from above the walls of the cave. The cave glistened with the reflected light. It was almost as light as being outdoors. I could see some of the Bigfeet watching me, but I did not see Earl. I wondered where he could be?

One of the Bigfeet had been left to watch me very closely. He was about seven feet, two inches tall and three hundred pounds. As he was coming closer, I stood up in the water. He was looking me over and talked with that whistling sound. I heard him, but didn't know what he said. He listened to me talk and turned his head from side to side, then grined showing his teeth. He laughed and reached out to squeeze my arm. I got out of the water and squeezed his arm. He laughed and danced around so I guess he approved of me. The Bigfeet are tall; they are approximately seven feet tall, short body, long legs and arms, a big chest, wide shoulders and covered with hair about five to six inches long. Their faces were clear with no beards. Their eye brows were set in a large forehead with a fine chiseled nose and a very pretty face. I went back into the warm water and it felt so good. I just lay there feeling better all the time. Then I started moving around to wash all the blood off. I discovered that I really needed a shave but I didn't have a razor. When I looked around, there was Earl coming toward me. He had something in his hands as he approached me. I could see that it was food. Earl reached out and handed me dried fish and salted beef. Boy, was that tasty. Then I needed a drink of water. But as I started to bend down to get the water from the lake, Earl stopped me. He directed me to a place where there was a small stream flowing near the cave. Earl leaned over to get a drink, so I helped myself, too. After I got my fill, I went back to the blue lake, laid in the shade, and ate some more fish and beef. After that I went to sleep.

Rock Throwers

When I woke up it was dark. I toyed with the idea of going back to sleep but since I wasn't sleepy I just sat and thought. Who was I? Why were the handcuffs on me and what had I done for them to beat me so badly? I just couldn't remember. Had my memory gone? Think! Think!, what did I do? What was my name? I just couldn't remember. All I knew was that my wounds had to heal and I had to get back. Maybe then my memory would come back. I remembered Earl throwing that rock. I had never seen such a thing; it was like a shot from a gun. I wondered if all the Bigfeet could throw like that? They could easily kill a man or beast. Earl woke me after I fell asleep again. He wanted me to take a walk with him. Well, one thing for sure, I certainly could walk better than yesterday and I didn't hurt as much. Earl took me to another part of the cave where we entered a room with water flowing through. This was their "so called toilet" and I used it as they did.

Earl brought me some more fish and beef, but this time he brought some kind of berries. They were very sweet and went well with the meat. I had another drink of water. After a bit, Earl wanted me to get back in the blue lake. The water felt good as I washed my face by cupping my hands and letting the coolwater run over my eyes. I could see better today and the swelling was going down and my eyes were almost open again. My legs felt much better also. There must have been some kind of healing power in this lake. As I lay there in the water, I saw other Bigfeet entering the lake. They too, took a bath, and relaxed in the water.

The Bigfeet are nice looking, very neat and clean, and seem to be very gentle. I got tired of laying in the water so I got up and started walking around trying to figure out where we came in. It started to get dark and I would have to come back another day. As I was leaving, I found another room which had broken guns, camping gear and other items lying around. I looked around to see if I could find a gun that I thought I might be able to repair. I did find a can of coffee and said to myself, "Ah boy!," I'll build a fire and have a hot cup of coffee. Since I had to have some wood to build a fire I waited until Earl left. I looked everywhere but I just couldn't find any wood. I put the coffee back into my suitcase thinking that tomorrow or the next day I would find some wood somewhere. The Bigfeet turned their heads from side to side for 'no' and up and down for 'yes', just like the human race. I discovered that the first night I was here. But, back to my problem. Why couldn't I remember anything? I knew all about how to brew coffee. As soon as I saw the coffee can, I new what it was and how to use it. Why couldn't

I remember my own name? I also knew about guns and how they were used. I knew the meat and fish that Earl brought to me was cut with a knife. So someone here was familiar with the use of a knife. They must have had a fire here somewhere to dry the meat and fish. Maybe I could find the place and prepare myself a cup of coffee. I was relaxing in the water when all of a sudden I saw several of the Bigfeet coming down the road whistling and screaming. I felt that I needed to get out of the water and run, but where would I go? Then one of them took me by the arm and took me with them. Where was Earl? "Hey Earl, I need help," I yelled. Finally, Earl came and made me understand that a Bigfoot was going to give birth and we all had to leave. He took me into the dark cave and I couldn't see anything; but Earl could see or he knew where to go because soon it became lighter. We went into a room where the sun was shining brightly. I was warm in there, almost too warm. This was where they dried their meat and fish and kept their berries. I didn't know what else these Bigfeet ate except grass. They were eating green grass and berries by the handful. They kept eating the entire time we were there. Earl showed me where they cut their meat into strips and laid it out on rocks to dry. They pounded berries into some of the meat before they prepared it to dry. It was a very clean area with no flies around. I wondered why?

Soon they all gathered around the new born baby and Earl wanted me to see the baby too. It was a boy. They look just like human babies, except he was larger. I would guess he weighed twelve to fifteen pounds. Then the Bigfeet started whistling, jumping and playing. They walked on their hands and did somersaults. All of a sudden, one Bigfoot picked up a rock and threw it across the cave. All the male Bigfeet went to the other end of the cave and started throwing rocks and whistling. I could not see the rocks until they hit the wall. They would put a mark on the wall, aim and throw. I had never seen anything like it. It was almost like shooting a gun.

The rock throwers joined hands and danced around in a circle. Round and round they went. It was beautiful. All of a sudden, there was a shrill whistle from the back of the cave and all the Bigfeet were quiet. The whistling turned into singing, like a whistling talk. It echoed through the entire cave. As I listened I could hear this beautiful voice coming from one of the female Bigfeet. Then it became very quiet and everyone started to leave. At that point I left too, walked back to the blue lake and went back into the water.

Bible

I felt I had to get hold of myself and find out whom I
was and get out of here. Maybe the suitcase will tell me
something. I picked up the can of coffee along with the
suitcase: if I only had a cup of brewed coffee and a fire. I
can't seem to find any wood to build a fire. I opened up
the suitcase and there I saw a razor, comb, soap, wash-
cloth, towels and a book. The Bible. "Oh boy!" Maybe
my name was in it. I opened it carefully and on the inside of the first page I saw a note, which read:

Dear Son:
Read and study this book. It is God's word. Live
by it and you will have a wonderful life. Pray
every day for one another. Bless you my Steve.
In Christ,
Your Mother

Steve: was that my name or did this Bible belong to someone else? I turned a few more pages. There it was: "Steve Lewis Yeager. Born March 21, 1924 in Calhan, Colorado. Weight: 8 lbs. 4 ounces. Mother: Lily Jean "Beek" Yeager. Father: Howard John Yeager, deceased. Killed by a bear at Dunton, Colorado in the San Juan Mountains."

"Wow! Was this my mother and father? Is this me or is this someone else?" I looked through the book and found no other information. This Bible was a gift from a mother to her son. "Could I be that son?" I was still lost. The names didn't help me recall anything. I still couldn't remember. I was feeling better now, but the back of my head was still swollen, I could feel knots on it. Maybe I had a concussion. Perhaps, in time, my memory would return. I went through everything in the suitcase and found nothing but pants, shirts, socks, shorts, towels, soap, razor, toothbrush, toothpaste and a small mirror. I looked in the mirror and saw that I really needed a shave but I still had too many cuts and bruises. I would have to wait a while longer.

It was getting late and nighttime would soon be here. I didn't like it but I couldn't go anywhere else. Earl had brought pine limbs and grass for me to sleep on. It was better than sleeping on the hard rock floor. I lay down and used a shirt for a pillow and soon fell asleep.

I woke up at dawn and walked around the large cave. It was so large that it took me awhile to completely cover the area. My legs were getting stronger every day. I decided to brush my teeth and then go into the blue lake again. The water was warm and I knew it would heal my body. There was something in that lake that gave a healing effect. I put my clothes on but not my boots because my feet still hurt.

Earl came to see me but he did not have anything for me to eat because he wanted me to follow him to the sunroom where they cook the meat on the rocks. Earl showed me a room with dried meat, fish, berries, grass, tree leaves and other plants. I could have anything I wanted to eat. I helped my self to the fish and meat. There were no flies in this room. I wondered why, especially with all this food. I really wanted a cup of coffee but I felt thankful to have some food. Earl left and I could not go back to the cave because I could not see. There were rays of sunshine peering through in places and it was very hot.

I really wanted to go outside, so I started looking around to find a way out. Finally, all of a sudden I was looking out on a beautiful valley. There were many Bigfoot lying in the sun. I walked outside in the open space where there was sunshine, open space, clean air, many trees, grass and birds.

I didn't have my shoes on so I couldn't go very far. But it was nice to sit down in the grass to relax. I fell asleep again. I wasn't asleep very long when someone shook me and whistled. It was a Bigfoot. He picked me up and ran behind the trees. All of the other Bigfoot were hiding. Then I heard it, there was an airplane flying over the little valley but I didn't know whether the pilot saw any of us or not. Everyone started to run toward the cave, so I ran along with them. I could not go back to the blue lake; I did not know the way. I wanted to go into the cave with the Bigfoot, but it was too dark to find my way in there. So I waited for Earl to come and get me.

Earl was a big fellow. He was over seven feet tall. He looked as big as a mountain to me. He came out of the eating room and gave me some more meat and berries. He was laughing and trying to talk to me. I talked back and whistled a song. He really liked that. He jumped up and down, whistled and danced around. Soon others joined, and they were all dancing around the small cave.

The big fellow took me by the hand and the rest of the Bigfoot followed. We went back to the big cave and the blue lake. The big fellow talked to me and I knew he wanted me to whistle; so I did. Bigfoot came from all over. While they were all dancing, one Bigfoot came up to me and slipped something into my hand. It was a harmonica. I stopped whistling and started playing the mouth-harp. It had a real nice tone and I played all the songs that I could remember. All of the Bigfoot went wild. They danced and jumped and did not want me to stop playing. After a lengthy spell, I ran out of wind and needed a rest. Where did this mouth-harp come from and how could I remember these songs? I still didn't know who I was!

Wolves

I didn't know how long I had been here. I had cut the chain of the handcuffs in two but I still had the cuffs on my wrists. They are hurting my arms and I must get them off. I went over to where the anvil was, found a chisel that fit into the square hole on the anvil, picked up the hammer, put the handcuff that was on my left hand on the chisel and hit it with the hammer several times. This cut the handcuff in two. But I still had the handcuff on my right hand. This meant I had to use the hammer with my left hand, and being right handed made things awkward. I still tried, but I hit my arm twice. This hurt, but I had to keep trying. Soon I had cut this handcuff off also. It felt good to be free. I was feeling better all the time. I wished I could remember who I was. At least I had a place to stay and plenty of food to eat.

It must be getting close to wintertime because the Bigfoot are staying in their caves more and the daylight is not as bright as it was. I was sure I had come here some-time during the summer. I wondered what these Bigfoot do all winter and what was I going to do? I fell asleep, but was jarred awake by all the noise that the Bigfoot were making as they talked to each other. I had to see what this was all about. A very small Bigfoot had come into the cave. He was about five feet tall and weighed ap-proximately one hundred-twenty to one hundred-thirty pounds.

He talked in that whistling sound and they under-stood each other. He was afraid of me and kept talk-ing to them. They tried to tell him not to be afraid of me. He started drawing pictures of the open plains and several ranges of mountains he had seen before he ar-rived here. He then pointed north, past the plains in the direction of Pikes Peak and indicated that that was the direction in which he lived. He then started talking and pointing at me. I thought he was trying to tell me that there were others like him looking for a new home. He moved about and kept pointing at the cave and I thought he was trying to ask if there was another cave that his people could move to. Bigfoot, the big one who was over seven feet came forward and talked to the little Bigfoot and nodded his head 'yes". He was going to take him to another cave. After the little Bigfoot ate and rested for a day or two they left. It was late in the winter before the big one came back. He was tired, dirty, and hungry. He spent a lot of time in the blue lake bathing. These Bigfoot hibernate during the winter but not all at the same time. It took awhile for me to figure this out. I thought they slept approximately ninety days. Earl had been hibernating for a long time now, so one of the other

Bigfoot had been taking me to the kitchen for my food. I could see the snow outside and it was getting colder. I tried to go outdoors but the exit to the cave was covered with ice and snow so I decided to stay in the cave.

I had not shaved since I arrived here and I had quite a beard. It was bothering me so I though I would cut it off. I got the razor and soap, and propped up the mirror. Bigfoot was afraid of me. I looked like a shabby beast. My beard was too long to shave with a razor so I cut it off with a knife. I sharpened my knife and then put the mirror against the wall and did my best to get rid of the whiskers on my face. I could see a scar or two but I really didn't look that bad after I washed my face with soap and water and got those whiskers off. Several of the Bigfoot were watching me shave. Then I took the knife and cut my hair the best I knew how. It sure felt a lot better and I looked like a man again. Even Bigfoot looked at me and smiled.

The days went by and I didn't know how long I stayed in the cave and read the Bible. Sure was glad I had this book. Bigfoot looked at me as I read to them. They listened but couldn't understand a word I was saying. I slept next to the blue lake, which was not too far from the anvil. All of a sudden I woke up and heard wolves howling. They were in the cave coming toward me and they were not friendly. I reached for the anvil and hit the anvil three times. These wolves were going to kill me if the Bigfoot didn't come soon. The King was the first one who came to my rescue. He screamed very loudly and the wolves stopped in their tracks. Other Bigfoot came and started talking to the wolves in that whistling sound. The wolves understood them and they understood the wolves. There was much rejoicing and love between them and they were glad to see one another. The King brought their leader to me and told him I was a friend. The big wolf came up to me, put his head down and licked my hand. I patted his head as he put his mouth on my arm. I then knew I was safe with the wolves. The wolves made marks in the sand and stayed with all of us for a long while. Bigfoot made marks in the sand and talked to the wolves about these marks. The King would point to some of the marks. He shook his head to indicate they should stay away from those areas. The marks in the sand were a map of this part of the country and the marks were the highways and for the wolves to stay away from. He also drew large open spaces with farms and ranch buildings showing where the cattle roamed. He told the wolves not to kill the cattle, only deer and elk. The wolves understood. The leader of the wolf pack would walk on part of the map and shake his head 'no' and then walk on another part and shake his head 'yes'. The wolves walked all over the map until they all knew where they could hunt and places that they should stay away from. There were fourteen wolves in the cave and I got to know each one. I loved them all. Earl noticed that one of the wolves was not very friendly towards me so he had him come over to see me. He showed me where he had been shot in the neck. The bullet had left a big scar that was covered by hair. Now I knew why the wolf shied away from me. I was really beginning to enjoy the company of the wolves. They were great animals and very smart. They all listened very quietly while I played my harp. When I played "Kentucky Waltz" in high "C" they would howl and nearly sing.

After awhile they began to feel more comfortable around me. We had a lot of fun with water fights in the blue lake. They would push me under the water many times.

I talked to the leader of the pack and he would listen to me. I told him I could not remember who I was and that I knew nothing about my past. I think he understood but could not give me an answer.

One day the leader came to me and held out his paw. I took it and started talking. He shook his head, as if to say no. So I stopped. He had a very sad look in his eyes and I knew they were going to leave. We shook hands one more time. Then he walked over to the anvil, stood on top of it and let out the most mournful howl that I had ever heard. All of the Bigfoot came and they knew the wolves were leaving. The Bigfoot sat on the floor and the wolves came to each one of them and gave them a hug. Then all of the wolves went into the cave and started howling. Their howls echoed all through the caves. It was a great sound. The leader then came up to the King with his paw and put it into his hand. They all walked out of the cave in a single file.

Boy! I sure was going to miss those wolves. I took my harp out and started to play slow, sad songs. I played louder and louder. Bigfoot listened but he soon wanted me to play something more cheerful. I did, and they began to dance and sing and soon everyone was happy. They sang and danced for hours. We were tired and finally we all went to sleep. Some of us dreamed of the wolves. They were our true friends.

No Coffee

I had been here a long while. I needed sunshine. After we ate, I went outside. Snow was still on the ground but I saw the green grass starting to come up. Spring was on its way. Boy, it felt good to be out in the sun. I saw some wood and decided to take a few small sticks with me so I could build a fire in order to make myself a cup of coffee. I picked up some small sticks about two feet long and took them into the cave. Soon a Bigfoot came and we both went back to the main cave. I picked up three rocks, arranged them in a triangle, put the sticks in the middle, put the water and coffee into the kettle, took out my matches and soon had a nice fire started. I was really looking forward to that cup of coffee. Oh no! Here came Bigfoot to spoil everything. They were afraid of fire and so fires are always put out. One Bigfoot picked me up and held me against the wall. They are very strong. The other took my coffee, kettle, wood and rocks and put them in the dark where I could not get to them. Bigfoot watched me night and day after this happened. They really were very afraid of fire. Somewhere in the past something must have happened to the Bigfoot. Some of them may have been burned. They kept watching me very closely.

Quite often when we went to eat, they would leave me alone for hours and I always wondered what went on in the big cave while I was gone. Something I was not able to see. I never saw many female Bigfoot. They stayed in other parts of the large cave where I had never been and the young ones must have stayed there with them. They probable came to the blue lake when I was outside with the male Bigfoot. I think the females and young ones would bathe and play in the lake when the males were not around and that was the way it should have been.

Panther

It was summertime now; the grass was green and the flowers were in bloom. The Bigfoot left me all alone so I went outside and started walking. Soon I was out of the valley and in the mountains. I could see for miles around but I still did not know where I was. I ate some dried meat that I had in my pocket. I kept walking and walking. There were a lot of pretty flowers, grass and trees. I even saw some deer and an elk or two. I also saw a porcupine waddling along. He wasn't afraid of anything. I looked up and there was a panther. I don't know how long he had been watching me. I was scared. I wanted to start back, but which way to go. I started walking away. There were some large rocks but no place to hide. So I kept walking, glancing back to see if the cat was following me. I could not see him but I was still scared. Maybe he was in a tree or behind a rock. There were very few places he could not climb. The only thing he would be afraid of would be a fire but I didn't have any matches and no way to start a fire. I must stay away from the trees, rocks and places where he could get above me. I didn't want him jumping on me.

It was starting to get dark. What was I going to do? Then I saw the panther again. I knew he was watching me. He could have killed me by now. I had no way of getting away from him. He just followed me. He didn't know exactly what I was and hopefully, he had eaten recently. Then I spotted a small cave. It was not very large but I could lie down and roll into it. That cat could still reach in and claw me. I wiggled and squirmed and got most of my body in the cave. I gathered some rocks around me. I held one in my hand to throw at the cat. It was dark now, but I could see the panther coming toward me. I threw a rock and hit him. He let out a scream and jumped on top of the rock and reached down trying to reach me. I smashed his paw with another rock and he let out another screech. Then he really came after me. I threw all the rocks I had and he still tried to claw me. I dug for more rocks and threw sand in his eyes. Then he backed off. I threw more rocks and sand. The panther was very angry by now. I hit him again. He was determined to get me this time. All of a sudden, I heard a different growl and something jumped at the panther. I strained to see. There was more than one: wolves. They drove the panther off and saved my life. It was so good to see those wolves. The wolves stayed with me the rest of the night and the next morning they took me back to the Valley of the Bigfoot.

Earl took me into the big cave and the blue lake. He sure had grown. He was almost as tall as his father. I decided to stay close to the cave unless one of the Bigfoot was nearby. It sure was a close call with that panther. I read the Bible and prayed often. I still didn't know who I was.

About twenty small Bigfoot came into the cave. They were tired, dirty and hungry. They all went into the blue lake and later another Bigfoot brought them food. They stayed about two or three days, and then the Big one took them to their new home, which must be far away. He was gone almost a month. The Big one was sure tired when he returned home. He listened but was not paying too much attention to what I was saying. We laughed, talked and belted one another on the arm. He wanted me to play the harp so I did. Soon the cave was full of Bigfoot. Even the females and the little ones came out and danced and played around in the cave. I liked the Big one. He could do things the others couldn't. He could reason and think. I talked to him and tried to understand his way of communication without success so I drew pictures in the sand of houses, barns and automobiles. He shook his head, indicating no, and started drawing pictures in the sand of deer, elk, and bears. He was big, but by his pictures he was scared of bears. He drew a picture of a very large bear; much bigger than any bear I had ever seen. Then he really surprised me. He drew a picture of a beautiful horse with a man in a saddle on the horse. The Big one stood up, took me by the arm and brought me closer to his drawing. He pointed to the man in the drawing and then to me and shook his head yes. I was dumb founded. He was trying to tell me that it was I on the horse. I said "no" and he said "yes". He had seen me riding a horse before I came in this cave. I was sure of it. I wondered how old this Bigfoot was? This Bigfoot was smart. If I could only understand him he could tell me about this entire country around here and everything that has happened in the last few years. I started drawing other pictures in the sand and he rubbed them out and shook his head no. He walked away and went into the blue lake.

No Flies

The wolves came again and headed straight for the blue lake. They played for hours in the water and did not want to come out. Earl came and we went to the kitchen to eat. Earl talked to the wolves but they did not want to come out of the water so we went back to the kitchen and ate more fish and meat. There was plenty of good food, including berries and other plants that I did not know about. They ate all of them. I tried the plants; some were good and some I could not eat. Earl took me to the area where they dried the meat. They had killed an elk and were cutting it in strips and laying them on the rocks in the hot sun to dry.

There were no flies. I was beginning to find out why there were no flies. The wolves headed straight for the blue lake. This was summertime; surely flies and bugs would be bad this time of the year. That was why the wolves stayed just a few days and spent most of their time in the blue water. If you bathed in the blue lake, there would be no flies or bugs and it would last for weeks. I loved these wolves. I talked and played with every one of them and was sorry to see them leave.

I went back to reading the Bible and again was wondering why I could not remember. Things like horses, flies, and everyday things came to me but who was I and where did I come from, especially with handcuffs. I just couldn't remember. Maybe someday something would happen that would bring back my memory. I sure hoped so. I remembered the name Earl. I remembered this boy, his name was Earl, but I couldn't recall much else about him. Yet, this young Bigfoot reminded me of him. I didn't know who I was but I felt good. I still had no coffee, but I had plenty of food. I got along well with Bigfoot as long as I didn't build a fire.

We went into the kitchen to eat and just as we arrived the other Bigfoot began screaming. Males and females were throwing rocks at a black bear that was trying to steal their elk. He didn't get any of their meat and left very quickly because of all the rocks that were thrown at him.

The Ancient One

I was sitting by the anvil one day, wanting to go outdoors but I did not know at this time what I would do or where I would go. I heard someone coming into the cave. It was not the wolves. They came very slowly and they were speaking in that whistling talk of the Bigfoot. I watched and soon I saw a tall, young, handsome black haired and blue-eyed Bigfoot. He was helping another Bigfoot who was very old, bent over, with white hair. You could tell that he had been a large Bigfoot in his time. I watched as they walked toward me. I stood up and the young one saw me but never stopped. I knew he was very important. The Ancient One came very close to me and looked into my face. He took both of my arms in his hands, talked to the younger one, and then nodded his head, yes. Then he gave me the largest bear hug that I have ever had and I hugged him back. I stared very hard at the Ancient One. He had a lot of lines in his face but his eyes were steel blue that just snapped and sparkled. This Bigfoot was someone "big", the Ancient One for sure. He probably knew all about Bigfoot. The Ancient One put his arm around me and we started walking. He said something to the young one who stayed by the anvil. We started walking and soon came to the blue lake. He motioned for me to help him into the water. So I did. He threw water on himself and in my face, then began to swim. He was a great swimmer under water and was having a good time. He talked to the young one who came over and got into the water also. He too was a good swimmer and a wonder to watch.

Soon we got out of the water and stood by the lake. I had a towel and gave it to the Ancient One to dry his long snow-white hair that hung in curls. He laughed and danced around, as he stood straight up while talking to the young one who was by the anvil. The Ancient One took me by the arm and we walked to the side of the cave. He nodded to the young one, who picked up the hammer and hit the anvil three times. He waited and hit it three more times. Bigfoot came from everywhere. But when they saw the Ancient One they fell to their knees and bowed their heads. The Ancient One talked to them as he held his hand out and they all stood up. He motioned for them to come. They did, and everyone hugged him. The big one came and hugged the Ancient One. He talked to him and he nodded his head yes. The big one went to the young one. They hugged and danced around. Then I knew that this was his son. They looked alike, only the young one had blue eyes. So his mother must be the daughter of the Ancient One. The big one came to me and wanted me to play the harp.

So I whistled a song or two, got my harp and began to play. They danced and played. The young one danced by himself then walked on his hands and did many tricks to music. Then all of a sudden there was a whistle and a high-pitched scream in the cave. Everyone became very quiet and this female began to sing. She sang very beautifully. We were very tired and soon all were bedded down for the night. I didn't know where the Ancient One had gone but they must have had a place for him.

Memory

Morning came and I walked around the cave. No one showed up so I went to the blue lake for a swim. It was great. I saw the young blue-eyed Bigfoot come across toward the cave. He had a bag over his shoulder and waved for me to follow. We headed to a part of the cave that had an opening but it was too dark for me to enter. The Ancient One was just inside the cave in the dark. They gave me a rope and started walking. I followed. It was dark and I couldn't see a thing. We stopped and I could hear water running like a stream. The young one left and soon a light came on way down in the cave. I could see the sides of the cave. Someone was coming. As he came closer more light appeared. I didn't know what kind of light these things were on the wall. The young one poured water over these rocks and they lit up very brightly. The Ancient One motioned for me to follow. So we walked over to the young one who lit the first light.

As we walked, the young one was ahead of us lighting up the lights. I could see drawings on the wall. As I went further, I could see more. The Ancient One stopped me and we waited until all the lights were lit.

We walked down to the last light. The young one had one of these lights in his hand. It was not hot; it just gave off light. They were showing me what was on the wall. The Bigfoot were all standing under huge trees. Then I saw a drawing of a Bigfoot and a giant bear. The bear was much taller than Bigfoot. The Young One and the Ancient One moved around and showed me how these bears had killed many of them. Next was a picture in color, beautifully drawn of a forest fire with large trees burning and animals running. The next drawing was a picture of dead trees, no forest and many dead Bigfoot and bears. They showed me how some of them made it through the fire and escaped into this cave. I wished I knew how long ago this had happened. I pointed at the drawing and asked the Ancient One if he was there. He shook his head no. The next drawing was of this cave and the only food they had to eat was the fish.

The next drawing really got to me. No trees, just little plants and some grass. Standing in this burnt ground was a thing standing on end. It looked like a huge bullet. What was this? Who made these drawings? Did they really see something like this? I stood in awe of this and could not understand. The next drawing was more confusing. There were four people with bubbles over their heads, talking to Bigfoot. The Ancient One pointed to the ones with the bubbles on their heads and started talking in that whistling tone. He pointed to his mouth, then to theirs. They taught them their language and that was what they still spoke. By the drawings on the wall, I could see that these strange people had lived here for years and showed Bigfoot how to plant trees, how to throw rocks, and how to dry meat. They also showed them how to love all animals and how to love one another. The next drawing showed the bullet shaped thing with fire shooting out of the down side and burning a hole in the earth. That is the hole above the blue lake. It shone, glistened and sparkled bringing all the light into the cave. That was the last of the drawings of the bullet shaped object and the people with the bubbles on their heads.

They had small drawings of wolves, birds and many eagles flying. They also had drawings of cliff dwellings, Indians walking with their bows and arrows. They had pictures of different tribes of Indians riding horses. The Ancient One stopped here and let me know this was where he came into the drawings. There were drawings of Bigfoot, many of them. One was taller than the others and had blue eyes. He pointed and knew that was himself. He sure was handsome, well built with steel blue eyes. Then came the miners who were digging holes all over the mountains. Bigfoot did not like this and were frightened by these people. So they hid from them and did not come out of their hiding. They had drawings of miners with guns killing all of the animals and cutting down all of the trees. There were drawings of buildings, small houses and small towns, people with wagons, many wagons with white tops traveling single file along the river. There were drawings of cars, roads, railroads and towns. There were drawings of many cattle, horses, people on horses driving cattle, people hunting and killing wolves. The Ancient One stopped and shook his head no. He did not like the wolves being killed. Then he pointed to people on horseback and then he pointed to me. I knew I was one of them. I knew about many of these drawings I saw on the wall and about the Indians and the covered wagons. I was trying very hard but I couldn't remember my name or why I was here. These drawings were really something. History goes way back in time. These people with the bubbles on their head; I didn't know about them, but something put that hole above the blue lake and made that water special.

I went back to look at the drawings of the bullet standing on end. I shook my head no and the Ancient One said yes. They were there. I went to the drawing that showed the burning of the hole in the earth and he shook his head yes; I knew this was true. I pointed to the big bear and made motions as to where they were. He made me understand they all were killed in the big fire. These drawings were done in color. Where did they get the color and how? I didn't know but they were beautiful. The wolves and eagles looked alive and the Indians looked as if they were just going to come right out of the drawing and walk right up to you. I pointed to an Indian in the lead on a painted horse and pointed to the Ancient One, wanting to know if he knew him. He nodded yes and tapped his mouth to mean he had talked to him. I pointed to a man in a later drawing riding a horse and driving cattle. I tapped my mouth, wanting to know if he talked to him. He shook his head no. He indicated they did not like him. I looked closely at this man. Maybe I knew him or he could have helped my memory. I did not know the man so there wasn't any help there. The young one was mixing paint, so I stayed and watched. He started painting huge airplanes, big ones with wings, windows and people getting into them. Some were taking off on the landing strips and some were flying overhead. He was painting with such ease. This took a long time and I was getting hungry and wanted something to eat. I made the Ancient One understand that I wanted to go back. We arrived at the rope, which led us back to the kitchen. Was I glad to get something to eat! The Ancient One talked the entire time we were eating. "If I could only understand him," I thought to myself. Later, he took me back to the blue lake and he returned to his drawing.

I wanted something to drink so I started walking back to the cave. I said to myself, if I only had one cup of Aunt Maggie's coffee. "Whoa! Aunt Maggie. Who are Aunt Maggie and Uncle Henry?" My memory was coming back to me. I knew who I was.

Aunt Maggie

My name is Buck Serajo and I live with Aunt Maggie. I work for her. I went to live with Aunt Maggie and Uncle Henry at the age of 9 after my parents were killed in an automobile accident when I was 8 years old. I love them both dearly. Uncle Henry passed away several years ago and I have been helping Aunt Maggie by taking care of the cattle and running the ranch. Aunt Maggie! Aunt Maggie! I have to get back. How long have I been gone? I know who I am and I know the two men who beat me. I've got to get back to the ranch. My aunt needs me. I hope Mac, George Macray, is still with Aunt Maggie. He helps out around the ranch. He is a good honest man and knows a lot about ranching. Aunt Maggie has helped a lot of people and I bet they are helping her now. Uncle Henry and Aunt Maggie have always helped people start their ranches. They would give them cattle and let them take years to pay them back without interest. They made sure that they had feed and hay for the cattle in the wintertime for the first year or two to get started. If they worked hard and really tried to get the ranch going there is nothing they wouldn't do for them. Many ranchers in this area got their start through Uncle Henry and Aunt Maggie. After Uncle Henry passed away, Aunt Maggie kept on helping people.

I have to get out of here. Where is the big one? I can make him understand. I have to find him. So I looked all around the kitchen and outside as far as I could see. There is still some snow on the ground but I can see green grass. I think it is Spring. I can't find the big one. Earl came and took me back to the blue lake. I tried to make him understand that I wanted to leave and that I had my memory back. But he just didn't understand. I packed my suitcase and I gathered my belongings. Now I know who Steve is and I know this is his suitcase and Bible. I have to find the big one. Maybe if I throw a rock he will come. I found a rock and threw it as hard as I could against the wall. No one came. So I throw another rock. Soon two Bigfoot came. I threw another rock. I knew they were laughing at me because I could not throw a rock as well as they could. They picked up several rocks and began to throw them. I don't know how they do it. It's the speed of a bullet and that is how they kill their deer and elk for food. Soon other Bigfoot came and started throwing rocks. I watched for the big one. Then I saw him. He was throwing rocks too. He could really throw rocks. He came to me and started talking and pointing. I think he was trying to let me know that the young blue-eyed Bigfoot was his son. The blue-eyed one came and picked up a rock and threw it too. Wow!

That was the fastest of them all. The rock no sooner left his hand that it had traveled the distance, which was around one hundred feet, almost instantly. I wanted to get the big one alone, but it would be awhile because they were still throwing rocks. They get very excited and I will have to wait until they calm down. After awhile, they quit throwing rocks and I got the big one by the arm and we walked to the blue lake where my suitcase was located. I picked up my suitcase and started to walk. I stopped and motioned with my arm that I wanted to leave. He pointed to his head and nodded, yes. Then I nodded yes. He knew that I had my memory back and danced and talked to the other Bigfoot. Some of them went to get the King, Queen and Earl. The King took my arm and motioned with his other arm, pointing out across the country and nodded yes; and I answered yes. They all gathered around me and grabbed my arm. Some of them hugged me. Earl had tears in his eyes and was happy that I got my memory back but was sad to see me leave. I picked up my suitcase and started to leave but they shook their heads no. The King put his hand over his eyes and closed them with a motion that we would leave when it became dark.

The big one wanted me to play the harmonica. As I was playing, the room began to be full of Bigfoot. They were all dancing, even the females. Then one, who could sing, started to sing. This was the first time I had ever seen her. That whistling voice was great. When she finished she walked over to me and gave me a hug and kissed me as she squeezed my arm. She then left. Earl took me to the blue lake. He wanted me to get into the water. So once again, I took my boots and clothes off and started swimming and having a good time. We played and swam for quite awhile. We then got out of the water and it was starting to get dark as I was dressing. Earl left and I was all alone. It soon became very dark and I could not see. Then big one picked up the big suitcase, and I picked up the smaller one as he led me away from the lake. He took my hand and we walked and walked but we were still in the cave. Then, all of a sudden, I smelled the trees and grass. I knew we were in the forest. Three others joined us, including Earl. We kept walking downhill surrounded by a lot of trees. We were still in the forest. It was a beautiful night but it must have been getting close to morning because the stars were becoming dimmer.

The next thing I knew, I was alone. Everyone had left and I would never see them again. Tears started to stream down my face but I thought about Aunt Maggie. She needed me. So I just kept on walking down the hill. The sun was up and it was beautiful county. I knew where I was but I still was a long way from home; at least twenty-five miles. I hadn't slept for over a day and a night. I had to get some sleep. I didn't want anyone to see me except Aunt Maggie and Sheriff Ben when I arrived back home. Needed to move on tonight. I found a pine tree, curled up under it and went to sleep.

Curls

When I woke up something was beside me. It felt like fur; and then it licked my face. It was the wolves. All of them were under the tree with me. I was glad to see them but we all stayed under the tree and we were soon asleep again. When I awoke the second time it was getting dark and the wolves were still with me. I hugged each one. Later, they left one by one as it became very dark. They left very quietly with no howling.

I left the suitcases under the tree, took the Bible, which had helped me get through the last few months, and started walking. If I walked all night and didn't get lost in this forest, I could be in the forest behind Aunt Maggie's house by sunrise. I walked and walked and soon came upon fences.

I knew I was getting closer. I needed to stay in the trees. I didn't want anyone to see me yet. I had been gone a long time and I had to see the Sheriff. It was getting daylight; I saw the glow in the east. I ran into another fence. This was the fence around the horse pasture just back of Aunt Maggie's house. I knew just where to go where I could see the house and make sure Maggie was alone. Look! There was the house, barns, and corrals. Tears came to my eyes; I wondered if Curls, my dog, was still alive. She was and here she came. I got down on my knees and she jumped right into my face, licking and kissing me for all she was worth. I was sure Maggie is alone. I started for the back porch of the house. I didn't want Maggie to see me until I was on the porch and knocking on the door. As I got near the door I knocked. The door opened and I said "How about a cup of coffee?" Aunt Maggie looked at me and cried and shouted, "Buck, Buck, where have you been?" She took me in her arms and we hugged and hugged. She wouldn't let me go because she just couldn't believe it was I. First thing, she poured me a cup of coffee. Man was that coffee good - it had been a long time. Aunt Maggie asked again, "Where have you been?" I told her the whole story from start to finish. She prepared me a meal of hotcakes, ham and eggs, and, of course, coffee. Then she baked biscuits and fixed sausage gravy - my favorite meal.

Maggie said, "Buck, I believe you and I know that Bigfoot were out there when we first came to this part of the country years ago. There were so many people in this area, miners, cowboys, and many others who depended on wildlife for food. Soon the game was gone and we had nothing to eat. One morning there was a string of fish hanging by our door. Another night I saw two Bigfoot hang half a deer on the back porch. I called Henry and he also saw the Bigfoot. Henry always said they helped gather cattle, especially in Dark Canyon."

She continued talking about the wolves and said it was hard for her to like them. They had killed almost all of the horses around here the first winter. Any horses that were not kept in the barns were killed or ham strung in the deep snow. They could not get away. The farmers killed every wolf they could find. Buck, you have told me where you were and that you lost your memory, but you haven't told me why Bud Clay and Steve Yeager beat you. "Maggie, they wanted money. They tried to make me tell them where you hid your money. I told them I did not know, but they did not believe me. They said you ran the ranch so Maggie must tell you everything. Bud Clay' kicked me many times and I believe he would have killed me. He was wearing a badge; he used to be a Deputy Sheriff. I was riding to Dark Canyon to look for cattle when I met Steve. I got off of my horse to talk to him when Bud slipped up behind me and hit me on the head. Suds, my horse, ran. I fell to the ground and passed out. They were throwing water in my face and when I came to I had handcuffs on my wrists. They threatened me and wanted me to tell them where you hid your money. I said, "I don't know."

Bud hit me and said, "You know where the money is so tell us." They beat me again and I fell. Bud started kicking me in the back of my head. I heard a scream. I thought it was me and passed out. When I came to again I was in a camp that was wrecked. The tent was torn down; all the contents were smashed and strewed all over. I passed out again. When I awoke I had handcuffs on my wrists and I could hardly stand up. I had to get those handcuffs off. "Aunt Maggie, I've already told you the rest of the story. I must talk to Sheriff Ben. Can you get him to come here by himself?"

"Buck, Ben is not the Sheriff anymore. Remember the young Deputy, Jim Stall? He is the Sheriff now. Buck, the two men that beat you tried to rob the bank in town, someone called the Sheriff and Ben and Jim were the only two on duty at the time. As they ran down the street toward the bank, they ran into the two robbers. Bud Clay shot Ben, and as he fell he shot Bud, killing him. Steve dropped to the ground, firing at Jim Stall. Jim fired back when Steve rose to see where Jim was and Jim shot him in the head killing him. Jim proved himself. Everyone saw what happened as Jim carried Ben to the doctor's office that day. Ben was laid up a long time. When he retired, Jim Stall ran for Sheriff and was elected. That was three years ago."

Maggie told Buck that she would ask Ben to come see him tomorrow. "By the way, Jim Stall married Jackie, Judy's younger sister. Judy never got married. She is still looking for you. Several other people have been looking for you, including Sheriff Ben and, his deputies, men, women, children, cowboys, miners, town folk, and merchants. They all roamed this country looking for you. Some are still hunting for you. Judy is still looking for you and she said you will be found alive."

"Maggie, have I been gone that long?"

"Yes, Buck, this is the fourth spring that you have been gone."

"What shall I tell Ben when he comes over? Can I tell him the whole truth? Does he know about the Bigfoot?"

Maggie told Buck that Ben had never talked about

the Bigfoot, except that he has heard the screams. "So maybe you can. He won't tell anyone else, but you will have to tell the rest of the people something. Buck, don't tell anyone about the wolves. If the people find out there are wolves here they will be running all over this ranch hunting for them."

"Maggie, what happened when Suds came home without me?"

"Buck, Mac put Suds in the barn and left the saddle on him. Then he called Sheriff Ben. He came right over and checked the saddle, blanket, bridle and Suds to see if there was any blood on anything. He asked a lot of questions. Mac said that you were headed for Dark Canyon so that is where they looked for you.

I am tired and want to go to bed. Your room is just as you left it. I will call Ben in the morning and have him come over to discuss this matter and decide what we want to do."

"I can't go to sleep. What will I tell Ben? I don't have to worry about those two men; they are gone. Maybe Ben will know how to handle it."

It's morning - I took a shower, dressed in my own clothes and went to breakfast. "Boy, I can smell that coffee." I gave Maggie a big hug and a kiss. It sure was nice to be home.

"Buck", Aunt Maggie said, "Sit down and eat, Ben will be here soon!"

What am I going to tell Ben? I'll have to figure that out when he arrives. I have known him almost all of my life. Maggie, you will have to let Judy know today; she has waited too long." Just then I saw a car drive into Aunt Maggie's drive. "Aunt Maggie, if it isn't Ben I'll go to my room." As I looked out of the window, I said to myself, "If that is Ben, he sure isn't moving around like he used to."

Ben came to the door and Maggie let him in. I was standing where he couldn't see me. Then I stepped forward.

"Buck is that really you?" Ben said.

"Yes, it's me."

Maggie told Ben that I had been gone for nearly four years. We shook hands.

"Where in the hell have you been Buck, we have scoured this whole country looking for you."

"Ben, two men beat me so badly that I lost my memory. They nearly killed me. I just got my memory back four days ago and walked home. Maggie will tell you what happened to me and where I have been."

Ben asked me who the two men were.

"You won't believe me, it was Bud Clay and Steve Yeager. One Bigfoot scared them off and destroyed their camps and took me to their cave. I have been living with the Bigfoot since then. They fed me and took care of me. I told Maggie the entire story. She can fill you in, but right now my concern is what are we going to tell the people? If I tell them about the Bigfoot, they won't believe it, and they will be swarming all over these mountains like flies."

Ben told me that he knew about the Bigfoot and was surprised that I had really lived with them. I told Ben how I lived with the Bigfoot and how I ate, danced, sang, walked and played with them. I told him how kind and loving they were and they wouldn't harm anyone. "Ben, I want to spend some time alone with Maggie and we don't want anyone to know about my return." I went to my room to rest and later Maggie called me to come into the living room to decide what we were going to do.

"Buck", Ben said, "We are going to tell the people that Bud Clay and Steve Yeager beat you and that they almost killed you. We will tell them that something scared them off and that you got away, lost your memory and lived in the caves in the mountains, and that you got your memory back all of a sudden. We won't tell them anything about the Bigfoot."

"That sounds good to me. I could have spent four years in the caves back in those mountains. Maggie, call Judy and have her come over, there is something I want to ask her. And Aunt Maggie, do I still have a job here on the ranch?" Tears came to Aunt Maggie's eyes, she cried.

"Buck, this ranch is yours. You will have to take care of me from now on. You will have plenty to do; Mac has his own ranch and will be glad to have you back."

Maggie called Judy. "Judy's coming over!" Maggie said.

Ben stayed and talked with Aunt Maggie while I dressed in my best clothes. I could hardly wait to see Judy. I returned to the living room and Ben had a big smile on his face.

"I have to meet this Judy. She has been all over this country talking to people trying to find you."

I saw a car driving up the road. It was Judy. I was nervous. "What will I say to her?" Aunt Maggie opened the door and there stood Judy. I ran to her, swept her into my arms and said, "I love you. I love you Judy!"

Tears rolled down her cheeks, she grabbed my face with her hands and started kissing me. "I love you. I love you too. Where have you been? I've missed you so much."

"Judy, Bud Clay and Steve Yeager tried to make me tell them where Aunt Maggie hid her money. I would not tell them so they beat and nearly killed me. Something scared them away and they ran. Then all of a sudden I found myself in some caves in the forest. I couldn't remember anything until four days ago when, once again, I was longing for a cup of coffee and all of a sudden Aunt Maggie and her delicious coffee came to my mind. So here I am."

I got down on my knees "Judy, I can't wait. Will you marry me?" Judy fell to her knees too and put her arms around me and said, "Yes, yes, real soon. Reverend Case will marry us in the church. I know just the wedding dress I want. After the wedding we can honeymoon in Mom and Dad's cabin in the mountains. Lets set the date."

Aunt Maggie said she would give us a reception in the high school gym because there would be too many people to hold it in the church hall.

"I want to be married in our church by Reverend Case and have the men dress in western suits and cowboy boots," Judy said.

I told her that would be fine with me.

"This is going to be one of the largest weddings this town has ever had," Ben said, with tears in his eyes. "I am going to go to the Sheriff and tell him the entire story. I am sure everything will be alright."

There was a knock at the door and when I opened it, there stood Mac. He looked at me once, and then looked again. He laughed as he walked through the door giving me a hug that nearly broke my ribs.

"Man, am I glad you are back. I saw all of the cars; I know Ben's car and thought Maggie was sick or something."

"It's something alright. Buck is back! Buck is back!" I said, "Mac, Ben and Maggie will fill you in on what happened to me. Judy and I are getting married and right now we are going to her folks to get things rolling."

We left the house and headed towards Judy's parents home and were they surprised to hear that we had made wedding plans already. Judy told them that we had set the date one week from today. Judy drove me back home and we began making plans for the wedding.

Ben must have told everyone. The sheriff, his wife, Jackie, Reverend Case and the president of the bank were among many people who stopped by to see me. Even the news reporters asked me several questions, which I tried to answer. I didn't know that I had so many friends. It was great.

Our wedding day arrived and the ceremony began just as it did during rehearsal. Only this time, I was standing before Reverend Case with my best man, Mac. We were dressed in our new western suits and cowboy boots. The church was full of people. In fact, there were so many people that some of them were standing outside of the church. The organist began to play the wedding song. Then there was Judy coming down the isle to me. She was absolutely beautiful. You could see that her father was very proud of his daughter. We recited our wedding vows and then Reverend Case pronounced us man and wife. We kissed and walked down the aisle and out of the church. Friends and family were standing outside, overjoyed with tears and laughter as they threw rice at us. Our reception was being held at the high school gym. Many family members and friends were there to help us celebrate.

You should have seen Aunt Maggie. She is in her late 80's but the way she was all dolled up; she looked like she was in her 50's. Aunt Maggie and Ben led us to a beautiful wedding cake that Aunt Maggie had baked. Judy and I fed each other a bite of cake as we laughed. Everyone was having a good time. The band started playing our favorite song, "Have I Told You Lately That I Love You?" Judy and I started dancing across the floor while others followed. Judy danced with her father and then I danced with Judy again. After awhile I danced with Judy's mother, then Jackie and others who attended the wedding. The dancing went on, but Judy and I slipped out the side door and left the wedding party and reception to leave on our honeymoon. Boy, was that automobile decorated! We love one another dearly.

Three Years Later

Judy and I built a house near Aunt Maggie. She had her 90th birthday and is still doing fine. She advised Judy and me not to hide our money but to put it in the bank. I have told Judy all about the Bigfeet and the wolves. I also told her about the drawings on the walls of the cave and the Ancient One and the Blue Eyed One. I have never tried to find my animal friends and I never will. I did herd cattle out of Dark Canyon and I believe they helped me. We have a son. His name is Cody. He calls

Maggie, Grandma and she is absolutely delighted. Yes, Curls, my cow dog is still with us and I still have Suds, the horse I was riding when I was attacked. Ben is still with us. I see him at least once a week. It's springtime. Now with the rains we are looking forward to a wonderful summer with beautiful flowers and blue skies forever.

The End